All rights reserved. Published in the United States by Sandpiper,
an imprint of Houghton Mifflin Harcourt Publishing Company.
Originally published in hardcover in the United States by Clarion,
an imprint of Houghton Mifflin Harcourt Publishing Company,
2004.

FIVE LITTLE MONKEYS™ is a registered trademark of
Houghton Mifflin Harcourt Publishing Company, and the monkey
logo is a trademark of Houghton Mifflin Harcourt Publishing
Company.

SANDPIPER and the SANDPIPER logo are trademarks of
Houghton Mifflin Harcourt Publishing Company.

For information about permission to reproduce selections from
this book, write to trade.permissions@hmhco.com or to
Permissions, Houghton Mifflin Harcourt Publishing Company,
3 Park Avenue, 19th Floor, New York, New York 10016.

www.hmhco.com

The text was set in 19-point Weiss.
The illustrations are pen and ink and
acrylic gouache.

Library of Congress Cataloging-in-Publication Data

Christelow, Eileen.
Five little monkeys play hide-and-seek / Eileen Christelow.
p. cm.
Summary: The five little monkeys try to avoid going to
bed by playing hide-and-seek with the babysitter.
[1. Bedtime—Fiction. 2. Monkeys—Fiction.
3. Babysitters—Fiction. 4. Hide-and-seek—Fiction.
5. Stories in rhyme.] 1. Title.
PZ8.3.C456Fj 2004
[E]—dc22   2003015426

HC ISBN: 978-0-618-40949-5
PA ISBN: 978-0-547-33787-6

Manufactured in China
SCP 10 9 8 7
4500616386

For a new generation
of little monkeys:
Asa, Andy, Vivien
Isabel, May, and Kyle
Sophie and Yelena
Theo and Lucia

FIVE Little MONKEYS
play hide-and-seek

sandpiper
Houghton Mifflin Harcourt
Boston · New York

The five little monkeys
are ready for bed.
Their mama's going dancing.
She's dressed in bright red.

"Lulu's the sitter.
You'd better be good.
No tricks! No silliness!
Is that understood?"

"We'll be good!" shout the monkeys.
"We'll play hide-and-seek!
Hey, Lulu, you're it!
And you'd better not peek!"

"Just one game," says Lulu.
"Then it's right off to bed.
Your bedtime's at eight.
That's what your mama said."

Lulu starts counting.
She counts up to ten.

7

"Where are those monkeys?
Where did they go?
Where are they hiding?
I really don't know!"

But wait! . . .
"I see some fingers.
I see some toes.
I see some eyes.
I see a nose."

"No fair!" shout the monkeys.
"You found us too fast!
Let's play one more game.
And this will be the last!"

"Hold on!" says Lulu.
"It's time for bed.
'No tricks! No silliness!'
That's what your mama said."

"Oh, *please*," say the monkeys.
"Just one game more?
And this time can you count
to at least twenty-four?"

"Okay," sighs Lulu.
She's counted to four
when those monkeys start sneaking
right out the front door.

13

"Where are those monkeys?
Where did they go?
Where are they hiding?
I really don't know!"

16

But wait. . .
"I see some fingers.
I see some toes.
I see some eyes.
I see a nose!"

"No fair!" shout the monkeys.
"You found us too fast!
Let's play another game.
And this will be the last."

"Hold on!" says Lulu.
"It's past time for bed.
'No tricks! No silliness!'
That's what your mama said."

19

1 2 3 4 5 6 7 8 9 10 11 **12** 13 **14** 15 16 17 18 19 20 21 **22** 23 24 25 26 2

But the monkeys convince her
to play one game more,
and Lulu starts counting
to one hundred and four.

28 29 30 31 32 33 34 35 36 37 38 39 40 41 42 43 44 45 46 47 48 49 50 51...

"Quick!" shout the monkeys.
"We all need to hide
in a place she won't think of
—somewhere inside."

21

...52 53 54 55 **56** 57 58 59 **60** 61 62 63 **64** 65 66 67 68 69 70 71 **72**

"Let's hide in the closet!"
"No, behind the chair!"
"No, under this table!"
"But she'll find us there!"

"Wait!" says one monkey.
She heads for the hall.
"I know a place
she won't think of at all!"

75 77 78 79 80 81 82 83 **84** 85 86 87 **88** 89 **90** 91 **92** 93 94 95 **96** 97...

23

Lulu stops counting.
She looks all around.
"Where are those monkeys?"
There isn't a sound!

She looks behind bushes.

She searches the tree.

26

She hunts in the closets.

Where can they be?

Under the table?
Behind the big chair?
Those five little monkeys
aren't anywhere!

27

"Come on, you monkeys!
  It's past time for bed.
'No tricks! No silliness!'
  That's what your mama said."

Lulu is worried.
"Where *can* they be?
  They'll never get to bed,
  and their mama will blame me!"

Just then, in comes Mama.
"Did the children behave?"
"They're gone!" Lulu wails.
   She tries to be brave.

"Gone?" says Mama.
   She scratches her head.
"I just peeked in their window,
   and saw them in . . .

"We fooled you!"
  shout the monkeys.
"Now, let's play again.
  Lulu, *you* hide,
  and *we'll* count to ten."

"No way!" says Lulu.
"You've got to go to sleep.
  But if you want to count,
  I'll help you count . . .

31

. . . SHEEP!"

7

8

10

9

11

And so they start counting.
They're up to thirty-four,
when those five little monkeys
all start to snore.

12. . . .

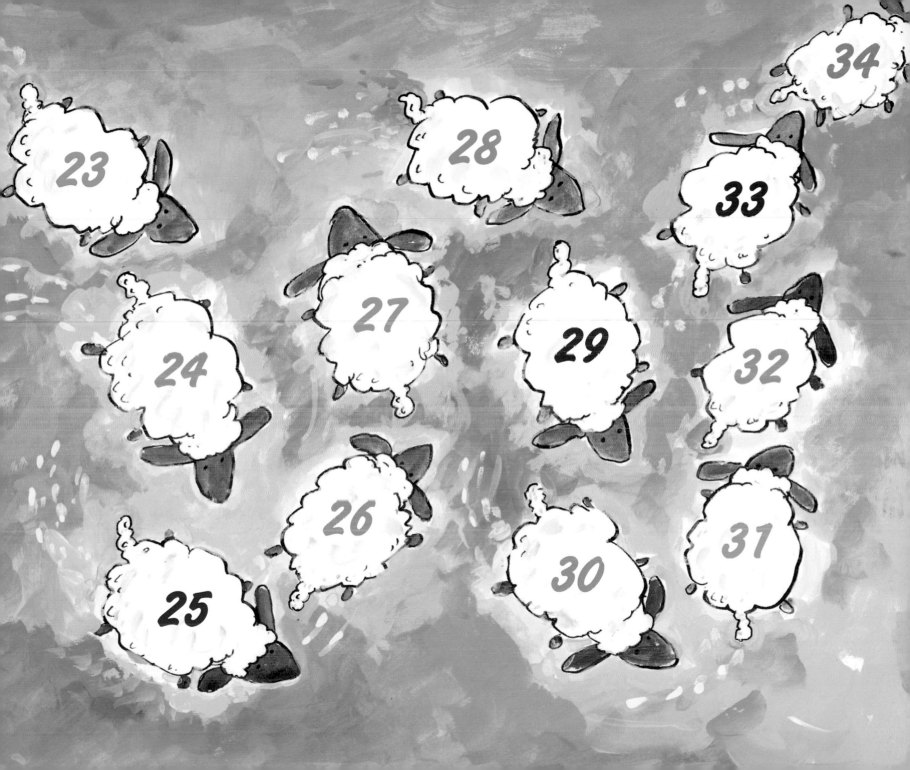